**14**
DAY LOAN

# Alison's Fierce and Ugly Halloween

## Marion Dane Bauer

### ILLUSTRATED BY
### Laurie Spencer

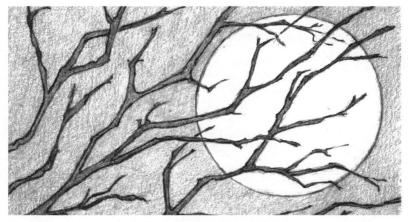

## Hyperion Books for Children
## New York

Other books by the same author:
*Alison's Wings*
*Alison's Puppy*

Holiday Colletion
T
Bau

Text © 1997 by Marion Dane Bauer.
Illustrations © 1997 by Laurie Spencer.

Printed in the United States of America.

First Edition

1 3 5 7 9 10 8 6 4 2

The artwork for each picture is prepared using pencil.
The book is set in 20-point Berkeley Book.

Library of Congress Cataloging-in-Publication Data
Bauer, Marion Dane.
Alison's fierce and ugly Halloween / Marion Dane Bauer ;
illustrated by Laurie Spencer.
p.    cm.
Summary: Alison dresses as a fierce and ugly pirate for Halloween, but she is disappointed and angry when everyone says she looks cute.
ISBN 0-7868-1211-7 (pbk. ed.)—ISBN 0-7868-2262-7 (lib. bdg.)
[1. Halloween—Fiction.  2. Pirates—Fiction.] I. Spencer, Laurie, ill. II. Title.
PZ7.B3262Ag    1997
[E]—dc20                                96-38547

For Katy Bauer, at last,
with all my love
—M. D. B.

# CONTENTS

CHAPTER 1 . . . . . . . . . . . . . .1

CHAPTER 2 . . . . . . . . . . . . .5

CHAPTER 3 . . . . . . . . . . . . .9

CHAPTER 4 . . . . . . . . . . . .14

CHAPTER 5 . . . . . . . . . . .18

CHAPTER 6 . . . . . . . . . . .23

CHAPTER 7 . . . . . . . . . . .27

CHAPTER 8 . . . . . . . . . . . .31

CHAPTER 9 . . . . . . . . . . .35

# 1

Alison loved Halloween.

She loved the scary stories.

She loved going out in the night, and she loved getting gobs and gobs of candy.

But most of all, Alison loved dressing up. On Halloween she could be anyone she wanted to be. Anyone at all.

One year she had been a ballerina.

1

Another year she was a fairy.

And after that she was a princess with a sparkly crown.

But this Halloween, Alison wanted to be a pirate. She wanted to be an *ugly* pirate. A *fierce* and ugly pirate. And she was going to scare everyone in town.

Alison had found a kerchief to cover her head.

She had bought a scar to stick on her cheek.

She had borrowed a sword with a bloodred point.

And she had made a black patch to cover one eye.

"You were such a pretty fairy," Alison's mother said.

"Don't you want to be a ballerina?" her father asked.

"I remember when you were a princess with a sparkly crown," her grandfather added.

But Alison said, "I am going to be a pirate.

"I am going to be a fierce and ugly pirate.

"And I will scare everyone in town."

Mike, Alison's big brother,

laughed. But Mike always laughed at her.

Even Mom and Dad smiled. But they hid their smiles behind their hands.

Grandpa said, "I just hope my old legs can keep up with a fierce and ugly pirate this Halloween."

Cindy, Alison's best friend, said, "I will be a fierce and ugly pirate, too."

**2**

At last, Halloween came.

The night was extra dark. Even the moon hid its face.

Dead leaves rattled along the walks.

And up and down the street, spooks appeared.

Ghosts and ghouls, fairies and princesses, space creatures and rock stars all came out to trick-or-treat.

Alison and Cindy put on their kerchiefs.

They stuck on their scars.

Alison picked up her plastic sword. Cindy held her treasure box.

And they each put on a black eye patch.

Then Alison filled her pockets with pebbles.

"What are those for?" Cindy asked.

"Pirates always carry ammunition," Alison said. "Just in case."

Cindy filled her pockets with pebbles, too. "Just in case," she said.

"Hurry!" Mike called. "Grandpa is ready."

Mike and his friend Noah were mummies. They were wrapped from head to toe in strips of white cloth.

But they didn't look a bit scary. They looked like boys in torn sheets.

"Yo, ho, ho," Alison and Cindy said. "We are fierce and ugly pirates. And we are ready."

Mike and Noah rolled their eyes.

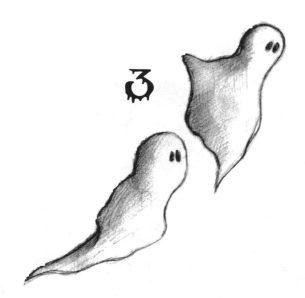

Grandpa stopped in front of the Carlsons' house.

The children ran to the porch. They rang the doorbell. "Trick or treat," they called.

The Carlson family came to the door.

"Oh, look!" Mrs. Carlson cried. "Mummies and pirates!"

Alison put on an ugly scowl.

Cindy scowled, too.

They scowled so hard that the Carlson baby hid his eyes. They even scowled at the Snickers bars Mr. Carlson gave them.

"What nice girls!" Mr. Carlson said.

"What *nice* girls!" Mike repeated. He and Noah ran to the next house.

Alison and Cindy scowled at the boys.

Mr. Rose gave out dimes. Alison waved her sword fiercely and Cindy waved her treasure box.

Mr. Rose smiled.

Mike and Noah shook their heads.

Alison and Cindy shook the sword and treasure box harder.

Mrs. Harvey gave them caramels. Alison wiggled her scar. Cindy tugged on her eye patch.

"Aren't you sweet?" Mrs. Harvey said.

Mike and Noah giggled.

"No!" Alison and Cindy said.

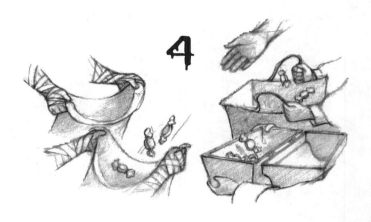

# 4

**M**r. Chang gave out small bags
of potato chips.

The boys said, "Thank you."

The girls crossed their eyes.
Alison even crossed the eye
beneath the patch.

But Mr. Chang didn't look a bit
scared.

Mrs. Betts had a bowl of
suckers. The boys each took one.

Cindy took two. Alison took three.

"Would you like some more?" Mrs. Betts asked.

Mr. and Mrs. Donati had chocolate coins. The coins were wrapped in gold paper. Just like real treasure.

Alison and Cindy turned as fierce and ugly as pirates can be.

They each grabbed a handful of coins and crossed their eyes.

Mr. and Mrs. Donati laughed.

Cindy wiggled her scar. Alison waved her sword and scowled so hard her face hurt.

Mr. and Mrs. Donati laughed some more.

The boys laughed, too. All the way to the next house.

"I think we aren't such fierce pirates after all," Cindy said.

"I am," Alison told her. "I am just as fierce as a pirate can be."

# 5

**M**iss Sheldon opened her door. In one hand she held a cane. In the other, she held a box of Twinkies. Even her smile seemed wrinkled.

"Trick or treat," Mike and Noah said.

"Trick or treat," Cindy and Alison added.

Miss Sheldon looked at Mike

and Noah. "Oh my," she said. "Mummies. How scary!"

The boys grinned. Alison held her breath.

Miss Sheldon looked at Alison and Cindy. "Goodness," she said. "Pirates. How cute!"

The boys' grins grew wider. Alison stamped her foot.

But Miss Sheldon was too busy handing out Twinkies to notice. And the boys were too busy getting Twinkies to care.

"Thank you!" Mike and Noah said. And they ran on.

"Thank you," Cindy said.

Alison didn't say a word. She just glared at the door after

Miss Sheldon shut it.

"Let's go," Cindy said. Alison didn't move. "We are pirates," she said.

"I know," Cindy answered.

Alison looked over at Grandpa. He stood under the streetlight. He

was talking to Noah's
father.

"Pirates are not cute," she said.

"I know," Cindy answered.

Alison put her hands into her
pockets. She rattled the pebbles.
She stared at Miss Sheldon's
porch.

"Pirates are very fierce and
ugly," she said.

Cindy said nothing at all.

**P**ebbles rained down on Miss Sheldon's porch. They banged and bounced. They skittered beneath the swing. They piled in front of the door.

"Your turn now," Alison said to Cindy.

Cindy put her hands into her pockets. She rattled her pebbles. She stared at Miss Sheldon's porch.

"Ready! Aim! Fire!" Alison said.

Cindy took her hands out of her pockets. "Throwing pebbles isn't polite," she said.

"You are a pirate," Alison told Cindy. "Pirates are never polite."

Cindy shook her head. "I don't want to be a pirate," she said. "I never wanted to be a pirate . . . really. I want to go home."

Alison looked at Cindy. Cindy took off her black eye patch.

Alison looked over at Grandpa. He waved and smiled.

Alison looked at Miss Sheldon's porch.

She thought maybe she wanted to go home, too.

"Come on, girls," Grandpa called.

Alison and Cindy came.

"Are you having fun?" he asked.

Cindy didn't answer. Alison didn't answer, either.

Grandpa took their hands. They walked along together.

"Look at that fine jack-o'-lantern," Grandpa said.

Alison didn't look. Cindy didn't look, either.

Grandpa checked their candy. "It looks good," he said. "Do you want to eat some?"

Cindy unwrapped a caramel. Alison unwrapped a sucker. She licked it.

The sucker tasted like a pebble. Exactly.

**7**

The next morning Alison didn't eat any breakfast. She didn't eat any treats, either.

"Too much Halloween last night," Mom and Dad said.

Alison went outside and sat on the front steps.

Cindy came over. "What are you doing?" she asked.

"Sitting," Alison replied. "I am

sitting on the steps."

Cindy sat on the steps, too.

"Do you want to play house?" Cindy asked.

Alison shook her head.

"Do you want to play school?" Cindy asked.

Alison shook her head again.

"Do you want to play pirates?" Cindy asked.

Alison said, "NO!" Very loudly. Then she stood up.

"I want to go for a walk," she said.

"Where do you want to walk?" Cindy asked.

"Around the block," Alison told her.

So Alison and Cindy walked around the block.

They passed Miss Sheldon's house.

They walked around the block again. They passed Miss Sheldon's house again.

The third time they walked around the block Miss Sheldon was standing on her porch.

In one hand she held a cane. In the other she held a broom.

"Just look at what some bad boys did," Miss Sheldon called. She pointed to her messy porch.

"Boys can be fierce and ugly," Alison said.

"Especially on Halloween," Cindy agreed.

"I know which boys did this," Miss Sheldon said.

Cindy looked at Alison. Alison looked at Cindy.

"They were dressed like mummies," Miss Sheldon said.

Alison looked at Cindy. Cindy looked at Alison.

"I am going to find out who they were. Then I will tell their

31

parents," Miss Sheldon said.

Alison moved closer to the porch. She cleared her throat.

"Uh," she said.

"You see," she said.

"Well," she said.

"I was a pirate this Halloween. I was more fierce and ugly than any boy."

Miss Sheldon looked surprised. Then she looked angry. Then she looked sad.

"Were you a pirate, too?" she asked Cindy.

Cindy said, "I think I hear my mother calling."

But Alison answered for her. "I was the only truly fierce and ugly

pirate this Halloween," she said.
   And, of course, that was true.
   Miss Sheldon looked at Alison
for a long time. Then she handed
her the broom. "I like my porch
to be very clean," she said.

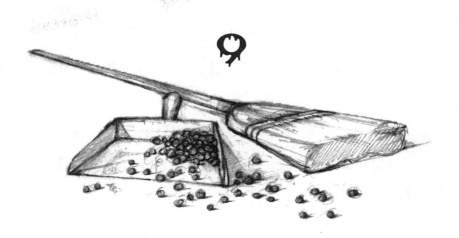

**A**lison swept and swept.

"May I help?" Cindy asked.

"Pirates clean up their own messes," Alison said. "Even the fierce and ugly kind."

She swept the pebbles into a pile. She swept the pile into a dustpan. Then she carried the dustpan to the driveway.

"Thank you, Alison," Miss

Sheldon said. And she smiled a slow, wrinkled smile. "Thank you very much."

"You are welcome," Alison said.

Cindy and Alison started down the walk.

"Alison," Miss Sheldon called.

Alison turned back.

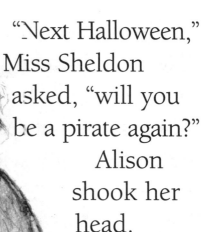

"Next Halloween," Miss Sheldon asked, "will you be a pirate again?" Alison shook her head.

"No!" she said.

Miss Sheldon waved a happy wave. The girls started for home.

"Next Halloween," Cindy said to Alison, "I am going to be a dancing fairy princess. What will you be?"

Alison thought for a long time.
"Next Halloween," she said finally,
"I am going to be a wicked troll."
She smiled at Cindy. "A very
fierce and ugly wicked troll."

# If you liked *Alison's Fierce and Ugly Halloween*, look for these books in your library or bookstore:

*Alison's Wings* by Marion Dane Bauer
If she wishes hard enough, will Alison's dream for her own pair of wings come true?

*Alison's Puppy* by Marion Dane Bauer
Alison wants a cuddly puppy for her birthday, against her family's wishes, and her grandfather may have the perfect solution.

*The Banana Split from Outer Space* by Catherine Siracusa
No one stops at Stanley Pig's roadside stand since the highway was built. Then Zelmo runs out of dinko blam and his flying saucer crashes down on the site.

*Edwin and Emily* by Suzanne Williams
Emily loves to play with her brother, Edwin, but sometimes Edwin doesn't want to play with Emily . . . and sometimes Emily doesn't play by Edwin's rules.

*Emily at School* by Suzanne Williams
Emily is sure she's ready to meet every challenge—and adventure—in second grade, but is second grade ready for Emily?

*The Peanut Butter Gang* by Catherine Siracusa
When the doorbells stop ringing, something odd is afoot in the town of Bellville.

# Read all the Hyperion Chapters

## 2ND GRADE

**Alison's Fierce and Ugly Halloween** by Marion Dane Bauer
**Alison's Puppy** by Marion Dane Bauer
**Alison's Wings** by Marion Dane Bauer
**The Banana Split from Outer Space** by Catherine Siracusa
**Edwin and Emily** by Suzanne Williams
**Emily at School** by Suzanne Williams
**The Peanut Butter Gang** by Catherine Siracusa
**Scaredy Dog** by Jane Resh Thomas

## 2ND/3RD GRADE

**The Best, Worst Day** by Bonnie Graves
**I Hate My Best Friend** by Ruth Rosner
**Jenius: The Amazing Guinea Pig** by Dick King-Smith
**Jennifer, Too** by Juanita Havill
**The Missing Fossil Mystery** by Emily Herman
**Mystery of the Tooth Gremlin** by Bonnie Graves
**No Room for Francie** by Maryann Macdonald
**Secondhand Star** by Maryann Macdonald
**Solo Girl** by Andrea Davis Pinkney
**Spoiled Rotten** by Barthe DeClements

## 3RD GRADE

**Behind the Couch** by Mordicai Gerstein
**Christopher Davis's Best Year Yet** by Lauren L. Wohl
**Eat!** by Steven Kroll
**Grace the Pirate** by Kathryn Lasky
**The Kwanzaa Contest** by Miriam Moore and Penny Taylor
**Mamá's Birthday Surprise** by Elizabeth Spurr
**My Sister the Sausage Roll** by Barbara Ware Holmes
**Racetrack Robbery** by Ellen Leroe
**Spy in the Sky** by Kathleen Karr

# Marion Dane Bauer

One Halloween my best friend and I went trick-or-treating with our pockets full of dried corn kernels, "just in case." Every single neighbor gave us treats, so no tricks were called for, but those corn kernels cried out to be used. At the very last house, no one was home. My friend and I looked at one another, threw all our corn onto the porch, and ran away. I wonder if she still feels guilty about doing that. I do.